Once upon a Bathtime

LIBRARY AND ARCHIVES CANADA CATALOGUING IN PUBLICATION

Hughes, Vi, 1943-
    Once upon a bathtime / by Vi Hughes ; illustrated by Sima Elizabeth Shefrin.

ISBN 978-1-896580-54-8

    I. Shefrin, Sima Elizabeth, 1949- II. Title.

PS8565.U46O63 2010   jC813'.6   C2010-903690-5

CATALOGUING AND PUBLICATION DATA AVAILABLE FROM THE BRITISH LIBRARY.

Book design by Elisa Gutiérrez

10 9 8 7 6 5 4 3 2 1

Printed and bound in Canada on ancient-forest-friendly paper. Manufactured by Friesens.

Printed in Canada by Friesens Corporation—Altona, Manitoba.
Date July 2010
Job# 56866

The publisher wishes to thank the Government of Canada and Canadian Heritage for their financial support through the Canada Council for the Arts, the Canada Book Fund and the Association for the Export of Canadian Books (AECB). The publisher also wishes to thank the Government of the Province of British Columbia for the financial support it has extended through the Book Publishing Tax Credit program and the British Columbia Arts Council.

Canada Council   Conseil des Arts   BRITISH
for the Arts   du Canada   COLUMBIA
                                      ARTS COUNCIL

To Isabella and Olivia, who love stories
everywhere, even in the bath –VH

For my mother, Flora Shefrin, who
gave me baths when I was little –SES

Vi Hughes

Once Upon a Bathtime

illustrated by Sima Elizabeth Shefrin

TRADEWIND BOOKS

Vancouver
London

Bedtime, bathtime, storytime—

In goes little Cinderella,
Sleeping Beauty,
Princess,

You.

Scrub clean for dancing at the ball.

In goes a bunch of magic beans.
Water carefully.
They'll reach the sky.

In goes a huffing puffing wolf.

Drop him down into the pot.
Save three pigs and their
chinny chin chins.

In goes a little jumping frog.
Help him find the golden ball.
With a hop and a kiss, he'll be a prince.

In goes little Goldilocks.

Wash and rinse that curly hair.
There are bears to visit,
bears out there.

Here comes sleepy fairy godmother,
Calling softly,
"Cinderella,
Sleeping Beauty,
Princess,

You.

Out of the tub now!
Clock's a-ticking.

Bathtime's over, stories too."

Out come curly Goldilocks,
The helpful frog,
The little ball.

Out come squealing little pigs,
The huffing wolf,
The magic beans.

Out comes little Cinderella,
Sleeping Beauty,
Princess,

You.

The day is done now, sleepyhead.
No time for dancing at the ball.

Time to find a bed to sleep in,
A bed to dream in,
A bed just right.

Not too hard,
Not too soft.

Not too big,
Not too small.

Time to say good night to all.

Bathtime,
Storytime,
Bedtime.

Little Miss,
Cinderella,
Sleeping Beauty,
Princess,

You.

roughout history in the midst of a pagan world,
uction of God's enemies. Babylon is all the ungodly
owers of the world.

Chapters 15, 16. God's Wrath

a peers into heaven and sees seven angels who will
en last plagues" that complete God's wrath (15:1).
d for his holiness and the vindication of his name
e when at last all nations must prostrate themselves
5:2–4). The seven angels now come to receive seven
filled with God's wrath (15:5–8).

and the angels pour out the bowls of wrath on the
Sores break out on the followers of the beast (16:2);
gs in the sea die (16:3); all the fresh waters turn to
); the sun flares and sears the earth (16:8,9); darkness
follow (16:10,11); finally demons are loosed to move
all the nations to gather for battle against God (16:14).
ther and assemble at a place called in Scripture Arma-
5,16).

terpretation of Revelation 15, 16. These are graphic
scriptions of what will happen on earth at the end
g tribulation period.
Interpretation of Revelation 15, 16. These are symbolic
l descriptions of final judgment.

Chapter 17. The Woman on the Beast

w shown the punishment of someone identified as
ostitute" who commits adulteries with the kings of
2). John sees a woman seated on the scarlet beast.
d in purple, laden with jewels, and drunk with "the
saints, the blood of those who bore testimony to
The angel explains the mystery, again identifying
he antichrist (6–8). Aspects of the beast with symbolic
explained. The seven heads are hills "on which the
(9–11). The ten horns are nations that will give their
o antichrist and make war on the Lamb (12–15). The
tified as "the great city that rules over the kings of
will in time be destroyed by the beast, who wants
on of all power.
terpretation of Revelation 17. The futurist identifies
bylon" as the religious aspect of mankind's final consol-
rists see a close relationship between a coming western

(God) announced to his servants the prophets" (5–8). John eats
the little scroll and stands ready to "prophesy again about many
peoples, nations, languages, and kings" (9–11).

The Futurist Interpretation of Revelation 10. The futurist sees
this as an interlude, preparing John for the final, bitter revelations
to come.

The Historicist Interpretation of Revelation 10. The historicist
also sees this as an interlude. However, the message is for the
church. It is a promise that God has not abandoned believers
as they wait for the final judgment, which will come at time's
end.

Chapter 11. The Two Witnesses

Now John is given a task and very specific time periods are
specified. These correspond with time periods in Daniel 9 and
12.

He sees Jerusalem trampled for 42 months (1,2) and two un-
named witnesses who prophesy for 1,260 days (3). They are divinely
protected from their enemies and given power to bring drought
and plagues (5,6).

When they have finished the work God set for them, "the beast
that comes up from the Abyss" attacks and kills them (7). The
world rejoices as the witnesses lie dead in the streets of Jerusalem
where the Lord was crucified (8–10). Then after three-and-a-half
days, they are resurrected and called up to heaven in a cloud as
their enemies look on (11,12). Their departure is marked by earth-
quake and destruction, which so terrify the survivors that they
acknowledge God's hand (13). This marks the passing of the second
woe (14). God is about to take his kingdom (15–19).

Futurist Interpretation of Revelation 11. The two witnesses are
unidentified, though sometimes thought to be Moses and Elijah
(cf. Matt. 17:1–13). They are real persons, who testify in Jerusalem
for an actual three-and-a-half-year period before being killed by
the antichrist at the end of the first half of the tribulation period
foretold in the OT.

Historicist Interpretation of Revelation 11. The three-and-one-
half-year period is symbolic. It is taken from Elijah's life and represents periods of affliction. The trampled-down Jerusalem symbolizes
false Christianity. The two witnesses are not individuals but repre-
sent the whole church collectively as filled by the Spirit. The death
of the witnesses symbolizes the church silenced by persecution.
The resurrection represents its ultimate vindication by God.

Chapter 12. The Woman and the Dragon

Now John reports a vision that appears in the heavens and is clearly identified as a "sign" (1). The vision is of a pregnant woman, about to give birth. A dragon (Satan) seeks to devour the child who "will rule the nations with an iron scepter" (2–4). The child is snatched up to heaven and the woman hides in the desert. Again a 1,260-day period is specified (5,6).

John then observes a war in heaven, in which Satan and his angels are hurled down to earth (7–9). Then a voice announces from heaven that "the salvation and the power and the kingdom of our God have come" (10). Satan is overcome but furiously strikes out "because he knows his time is short" (11,12).

The dragon seeks to destroy the woman who gave birth to the child, but she is safely hidden by God (13–16). The raging dragon turns to make open war on those who "hold to the testimony of Jesus" (12:17–13:1).

Futurist Interpretation of Revelation 12. In the drama acted out here Satan and Christ are clearly identified. The woman who gave the child birth represents the Jewish people, who will be preserved during the last half of the tribulation (1,260 days) foretold by Daniel. The hostility of Satan, shown throughout history in anti-Semitism, is directed against all believers in fiercest persecution during this final period of world history.

Historicist Interpretation of Revelation 12. The historicist also sees the woman as Israel, the idealized church of the OT. The war in heaven is a picture of Jesus' victory on Calvary. Thus this chapter begins yet another recapitulation of the repeated message of this book, using different symbols. The chapter teaches that in spite of the hatred of Satan, the church will be preserved.

Chapter 13. The Beast from the Sea

Now John watches as a horned beast emerges from the sea (1). His shape reflects the form given Gentile world powers in Daniel 7. This beast is energized by Satan and followed by a worshiping world (2–4).

Again the 42-month period is specified. During it the beast holds power and makes war on the saints (5–10).

John then sees another beast, emerging this time from the earth. He resembles a lamb but speaks like the dragon (11). He performs miracles to authenticate the claims of the first beast (12–14) and forces the people of the beast to worship his image (15–17). The "number" of this beast is given as 666.

Futurist Interpretation of Revela[...] two more individuals. These are k[...] play key roles in the great tribul[...] first beast is believed by futurists t[...] 2). He will link the Common Ma[...] or governments) to form a unity [...] old Roman Empire. The second bea[...] with Satan they form a mocking [...] Son, and Holy Spirit.

Historicist Interpretation of Rev[...] the chapter as a symbolic exposition [...] The first beast is thought to repres[...] which emerge from the surging hum[...] sents false religion and false teache[...] of the divine revelation (the signifi[...] represents the entire gospel age.

Chapter 14. The Ho[...]

John's next impression is of the [...] standing on Mount Zion (1). The [...] honored for their total commitmen[...]

At this point three angels are se[...] humanity the good news (gospel) t[...] come (6,7). The second announces [...] (8). The third announces the endl[...] who worship the beast and exhorts [...] of the saints (9–13). Here a voice fr[...] ing a blessing on the dead "who d[...] (13).

When John looks up, he sees a f[...] a cloud (14). Angels, equipped for [...] gathering and the trampling out b[...] the city for a distance of some 180 [...]

The Futurist Interpretation of Re[...] this vision as an overview, or previ[...] The details are developed in subsec[...] Great" speaks of consolidated polit[...] the antichrist in the last days, wit[...] throughout Scripture Babel (Gen. 1[...] unification and world empire.

The Historicist Interpretation of [...] sees Revelation 14 as another paral[...] The elements in this chapter are tak[...]

the church [...] and the dest[...] and unholy [...]

Again Joh[...] bear the "se[...] God is prais[...] that will con[...] before him ([...] golden bowl [...]

On comm[...] earth (16:1)[...] all living thi[...] blood (16:4–[...] and anguish [...] the leaders o[...] The armies g[...] geddon (16:[...]

Futurist I[...] but literal d[...] of the comi[...]

Historicis[...] and not lite[...]

John is r[...] the "great [...] the earth ([...] She is dress[...] blood of th[...] Jesus" (3–6[...] the beast as [...] meaning ar[...] woman sits[...] sovereignty [...] woman, ide[...] the earth," [...] sole posses[...]

Futurist [...] "mystery B[...] idation. Fu[...]

political alliance and a western "one-world" religion. The overthrow of the religious power comes when the civil government overthrows the state church, to institutionalize worship of the antichrist.

Historicist Interpretation of Revelation 17. The historicist identifies the woman as pseudospiritual powers that operate in the world today.

Chapter 18. The Fall of Babylon

Now an angel with great authority shouts out his announcement. Babylon the Great has fallen (1–3). In counterpart, a voice from heaven calls on God's people to "come out of her," for she is doomed to be consumed by fire (4–8). The kings and merchants of the earth who profited from relationship with Babylon will mourn (9–20). But Babylon will be overthrown with great violence (21–24). Of particular note is the repeated phrase "in a single hour" (cf. vv. 8,10,17,19). The destruction of Babylon will be swift and complete.

Futurist Interpretation of Revelation 18. Babylon here represents the civil, secular, and military power of the nations consolidated under the antichrist. This union is to be destroyed by direct acts of judgment by God.

Historicist Interpretation of Revelation 18. The historicist sees "Babylon" as the symbolic representation of all past, present, and future centers of materialistic human culture. Christians are not to allow themselves to be seduced by Babylon, but to be separate, for all Babylons will be destroyed in God's judgment.

Chapter 19. Christ the Conqueror

The final sequence is about to be played out. John hears the massed, triumphant shout of heavenly multitudes, praising God for his victory over the great prostitute (1–5, cf. Rev. 17). He then hears a joyous announcement: God reigns, and the "wedding of the Lamb" has come at last (6–10).

At this, heaven stands open and Christ appears as a rider on a white horse, with the armies of heaven following him (11–16). The birds are called to come, to feast on the flesh of the armies gathered to war against God. In the clash which follows the earthly armies are destroyed, and beast and false prophet thrown "alive into the fiery lake of burning sulphur" (17–21).

Futurist Interpretation of Revelation 19. The futurist relates chapters 19 and 20 to the sequence of events found in the OT prophets.

Particularly relevant to them are Daniel 11, Ezekiel 38 and 39, and Zechariah 14. Chapter 19 is understood to depict the consummation toward which history has been moving, when Christ will rule with a rod of iron as King of kings. The "marriage supper" speaks of the consummation of our salvation, when we are at last revealed in our full glory as God's children (cf. 1 John 3:1,2). The battle described actually will take place, and the beast and the false prophet will be assigned to eternal torment before the last judgment.

The Historicist Interpretation of Revelation 19. The historicist sees typical apocalyptic symbolism in this passage. The overall picture symbolizes the complete victory of Christ and the total overthrow of all God's enemies. The beast and the false prophet are not individuals, but personified representations of Satan's power.

Chapter 20. Satan and the Last Judgment

This chapter picks up and continues from chapter 19. Satan is said to be chained in the Abyss, captive there for a thousand years, and unable to deceive the nations any more (1–3). Those who were martyred during the rule of the beast "came to life and reigned with Christ a thousand years" in a "first resurrection" which is distinct from the final resurrection (4–6). After the thousand-year period has passed, Satan is released. He again succeeds in deceiving the nations which surround Jerusalem to war against God's people (7–9). The last rebellion is as futile as the rest. Fire from heaven destroys the armies, and the devil is thrown into the lake of burning sulphur to be "tormented day and night for ever and ever" (9,10).

Then the ultimate comes. The physical universe dissolves, and all the dead are called to stand before God. Those not written in the Book of Life are judged "according to what they had done as recorded in the books." All whose names are not written in the Book of Life fall short, and are condemned to the lake of fire (11–15).

Futurist Interpretation of Revelation 20. The futurist continues to take these descriptions in their plain sense. The thousand-year period is taken literally and linked with many OT prophecies which speak of a messianic rule on earth. The two resurrections are taken literally and viewed as in harmony with teaching in both testaments (cf. Dan. 12:3; 1 Thess. 4:13–18). The release of Satan as well as his binding is understood to actually take place, as is the final battle. All this the futurist believes is necessary if God is going to fulfill his word as spoken through the OT prophets (cf. *Old Testament Eschatology,* p. 372, 373). Only then will the end described in 20:11–15 and 2 Peter 3:3–13 take place.

Historicist Interpretation of Revelation 20. The historicist takes this chapter as the beginning of the seventh and last parallel vision in Revelation. Like the others, it portrays the entire period between the first and second comings of Christ. The futurist argues that the "binding"of Satan took place at the birth of Jesus (cf. Col. 2:15). This is what has made possible the preaching of the gospel in our age. The thousand-year period is symbolic of the believer's present exaltation in Christ, which is a "resurrection" in the symbolic sense of that exaltation. The loosing of Satan refers to the end times. The final part of the chapter describes the one and only general resurrection, which will take place at the end of time.

Chapter 21. The New Jerusalem

John now sees a fresh creation, with a new heavens and earth. A New Jerusalem, made of jewels and transparent gold, some 1400 miles square, drifts in the sky over the refashioned earth. This is the inheritance of the children of God, who are purged forever from all the wickedness which doomed the unbelieving to the fiery lake of burning sulphur.

The city contains no temple. None is needed, for the Lord God Almighty and the Lamb are there, and all mankind will walk in the light their presence sheds. Peopling this new universe are those whose names are written in the Lamb's Book of Life.

Futurist Interpretation of Revelation 21. The futurist believes this to be a portrait of eternity and that all the redeemed are to share in that freshly created, sinless universe.

Historicist Interpretation of Revelation 21. The historicist agrees that the chapter gives a picture of the new heavens and earth. The elements of the description are still, however, to be taken symbolically. Thus the New Jerusalem is not a city but a symbol of the Triumphant Church, while the "new" universe is the present universe cleansed of sin and rejuvenated.

Chapter 22. Jesus Is Coming

A final vision of the new heavens and earth reveals a crystal river, flowing from God's throne. Its current carries it down the middle of the great street of the city, watering trees whose fruit and leaves mean healing for once-cursed humanity. The redeemed will walk in this city of God, serving him, seeing his face. In the light shed by his presence they will rule with him, forever and ever.

The vision ends with promise. "These words are trustworthy and true. The Lord, the God of the spirits of the prophets, sent his angel to show his servants the things that must soon take place" (v. 6).

John concludes his report, communicating both a warning and a promise. Jesus announces, "Behold, I am coming soon!" The blessings of this book are carefully reserved for all who have washed their robes (in the blood of the Lamb). All still tainted by sin will forever remain "outside."

The last words of the book, which are the last words of our Bible, sum up the hope of Christians throughout the ages.

"Yes, I am coming soon," sounds the promise.

And all the saints gladly reply:

"Amen. Come, Lord Jesus."

Reading Revelation

Because of the controversy associated with this majestic last book of the Bible, the main interpretive views accepted today have been outlined with each chapter. It would, however, be a mistake to become so involved in controversy over interpretations that we miss the impact of what Revelation unveils. The vivid portraits of sin and judgment drive home the fact that, for all its domination of our senses, this world is not the ultimate reality. A time is coming, soon, when God will act. By saturating ourselves in the apocalyptic visions of that time we can gain a healthy perspective on our present lives, and gain help in clarifying our values.

How can we best gain such perspective? Simply by reading through, and reading through again, the Book of Revelation. The final interpretation of many points may not be clear. But our awareness of the nature of what is to come will grow, and with it will come a purification of our lives.

Bible Weights and Measures

In modern versions such as the NIV biblical terms are typically translated into modern equivalents. Thus Luke's reference to sixty furlongs ("stadions") becomes "seven miles" (Luke 24:13), and John's two hundred cubits becomes a "hundred yards" (John 21:8). This is fortunate, as different cultures in OT and NT times had varying systems of weights and measures. In general however, the standards shown below reflect the system used in OT and NT times in Bible lands.

Linear Measures

Reed	6 cubits	8 feet, 9 inches
Cubit	6 handsbreadths	17.5 inches
Span	½ cubit	8.75 inches
Handbreadth	⅙ cubit	2.9 inches
Finger		.73 inches
Great Cubit*		20.5 inches

* used of Ezekiel's temple

Liquid Measures

Homer	10 baths	58.1 gallons
Bath	6 hins	5.8 gallons
Hin	12 logs	3.5 quarts
Log		.67 pints

Dry Measures

Homer	10 ephahs or baths	5.16 bushels
Letek	½ homer	2.58 bushels
Ephah	10 serahs	½ bushel
Serah	3½ omers	⅔ peck
Omer		2.9 quarts
Qub		1.16 quarts

Measures of Weight

Talent	3,000 shekels	75.6 pounds
Mina	50 shekels	1.26 pounds
Shekel		.403 ounces
Pim	⅔ shekels	
Grain	¹⁄₂₀ shekel	

Money

In the NT money is measured by weight, with the value depending on the metal used. Thus a talent of gold (75.6 pounds of gold) is worth more than a talent of silver (75.6 pounds of silver). The two most common NT coinage words, drachma and denarius, each represents a day's wage, and is often translated as a "silver coin."

The Meaning of Familiar Bible Names
Men

Name	Meaning	Key Verse
Aaron	Mountain of Strength	Exodus 4:16
Abel	Meadow	Hebrews 11:4
Abner	Father of Light	1 Samuel 14:50,51
Abraham	Father of a Multitude	Romans 4:16
Absalom	Father of Peace	2 Samuel 15:13,14
Adam	Of the Earth	Genesis 1:27
Ahab	Father's Brother	1 Kings 21:4
Ahaz	Jehovah Sustains	2 Kings 8:18
Alexander	Defender	Mark 15:21
Amos	Burden Bearer	Amos 7:14
Ananias	Jehovah is Gracious	Acts 9:10
Andrew	Manliness	Matthew 4:18
Aquila	Eagle	Acts 18:26
Barnabas	Son of Consolation	Acts 4:36
Bartholomew	Son of Tolmi	Matthew 10:3
Baruch	Blessed	Jeremiah 45:5
Benjamin	Son of the Right Hand	Genesis 35:18
Boaz	Fleetness	Ruth 2:13
Cain	Acquisition	Hebrews 11:4
Caleb	Bold	Numbers 13:30
Cornelius	Beam of the Sun	Acts 10:2
Dan	He that judges	Exodus 31:6
Daniel	God is my Judge	Daniel 1:8
David	Beloved	1 Samuel 13:14
Eli	My God	1 Samuel 3:13
Elijah	God is Jehovah	1 Kings 17:20
Elisha	God is Savior	1 Kings 19:20,21
Esau	Hairy	Hebrews 12:16
Ezekiel	God is strong	Ezekiel 3:22
Ezra	My helper	Ezra 7:10
Felix	Prosperous	Acts 23:24
Festus	Joyful	Acts 24:27
Gideon	Great warrior	Judges 6:27
Habakkuk	Love's embrace	Habakkuk 3:19
Haggai	Festival	Haggai 2:4
Herod	Son of the hero	Matthew 2:16
Hezekiah	Jehovah is strength	2 Kings 18:5
Hosea	Jehovah is help	Hosea 3:1
Isaac	Laughing one	Hebrews 11:17
Isaiah	Jehovah is salvation	Isaiah 6:7,8
Israel	Ruling with God	Genesis 32:28
Jacob	Supplanter	Genesis 27:36
James	Supplanter	Matthew 17:1
Jason	Healing	Romans 16:21
Jeremiah	Jehovah is high	Jeremiah 1:4

Name	Meaning	Key Verse
Jethro	Excellence	Exodus 18:9
Joab	God is a good Father	2 Samuel 2:28
Job	He who weeps	Job 1:8
Joel	The Lord is God	Joel 2:28,29
Jonathan	The Lord gave	1 Samuel 14:6
Joseph	May God increase	Genesis 39:2,4
Joshua	God is salvation	Joshua 24:31
Josiah	Jehovah supports	2 Chronicles 34:33
Jude	Praise	Jude 1
Levi	Joined	Luke 5:29
Lot	Concealed	Genesis 14:12
Malachi	Messenger of Jehovah	Malachi 3:16,18
Mark	Polite	1 Peter 5:13
Matthew	Gift of Jehovah	Matthew 9:9
Micah	Who is like Jehovah	Micah 3:8
Mordecai	Little man	Esther 10:3
Moses	Drawn forth	Hebrews 11:24,25
Nathan	He has given	2 Samuel 12:13
Nathanael	Gift of God	John 1:47
Nehemiah	Jehovah has consoled	Nehemiah 5:16
Noah	Rest	Hebrews 11:7
Obadiah	Worshiper of the Lord	1 Kings 18:13
Paul	Little	1 Corinthians 12:8
Peter	Rock, or Stone	1 Peter 5:2
Philemon	Friendly	Philemon 1
Philip	Warrior	John 1:43
Samson	Strong	Hebrews 11:32
Samuel	Asked of God	1 Samuel 3:19,20
Saul	Demanded	1 Samuel 13:12,13
Silas	Lover of words	Acts 16:25
Simeon	Hearing with acceptance	Judges 1:1–3
Simon	Hearing	Luke 6:15
Solomon	Peaceable	1 Kings 3:9
Stephen	Wreath, or crown	Acts 6:5
Thomas	Twin	John 11:16
Timothy	Honored of God	Philippians 2:22
Titus	Honorable	Titus 1:4
Zechariah	Jehovah remembers	Zechariah 1:3

Women

Name	Meaning	Key Verse
Abigail	Cause of joy	1 Samuel 25:3
Adah	Adornment, beauty	Genesis 4:20
Anna	Favor, or Grace	Luke 2:37
Bathsheba	Seventh daughter	2 Samuel 11:2
Bernice	Victorious	Acts 26:30
Candace	Queen	Acts 8:27
Chloe	Green herb	1 Corinthians 1:10
Claudia	Lamb	2 Timothy 4:21
Damaris	Heifer	Acts 17:34
Deborah	Bee	Hebrews 11:32–34

Name	Meaning	Key Verse
Delilah	Delicate, dainty	Judges 16:5
Dinah	Justice	Genesis 34
Dorcas	Gazelle	Acts 9:36
Elisabeth	Worshiper of God	Luke 1:41,42
Elisheba	God is her oath	Exodus 6:23
Esther	Star of hope	Esther 4:14
Eunice	Happy victory	2 Timothy 3:14,15
Euodias	Good journey	Philippians 4:2
Eve	Woman	Genesis 2:23
Hagar	Fugitive	Galatians 4:24,25
Hannah	Gracious	1 Samuel 1:27,28
Huldah	Weasel	2 Chronicles 34:22
Jael	Gazelle	Judges 5:6
Jemima	A little dove	Job 42:14
Jerioth	Tent curtains	1 Chronicles 2:18
Jezebel	Chaste	1 Kings 16:31
Joanna	The Lord is grace	Luke 8:1–3
Judith	The praised one	Genesis 26:34
Julia	Curly haired	Romans 16:15
Leah	Wearied	Genesis 29:17
Lois	Desirable	2 Timothy 1:5
Lydia	Bending, willowy	Acts 16:12–15
Martha	Lordly	John 12:1–3
Mary	Troubled, bitter	Luke 1:30
Mehetabel	Whom God makes happy	1 Chronicles 1:50
Michal	Who is like Jehovah?	1 Samuel 18:28
Miriam	Bitterness	Exodus 15:20,21
Naomi	Pleasantness of Jehovah	Ruth 4:14,15
Orpah	Fawn	Ruth 1:4
Persis	Taken by storm	Romans 16:12
Phoebe	Pure as the moon	Romans 16:1,2
Priscilla	Simplicity	Romans 16:3
Rachel	Lamb	Genesis 29:17
Rebecca	Captivating	Genesis 24:67
Rhoda	Rose	Acts 12:13,14
Ruth	Affectionate	Ruth (book of)
Sapphira	Beautiful	Acts 5:9
Sarah	Princess	Hebrews 11:11
Susanna	White lily	Luke 8:2,3
Tamar	Palm tree	Ezekiel 48:28
Tirzah	Pleasantness	Numbers 26:33

Miracles Recorded in the Old Testament

1. The flood ...... Gen. 7, 8
2. Destruction of Sodom and Gomorrah 19:24
3. Lot's wife turned into a "pillar of salt" 19:26
4. Birth of Isaac at Gerar 21:1
5. The burning bush not consumed .... Ex. 3:3
6. Aaron's rod changed into a serpent 7:10-12
7. The ten plagues of Egypt—(1) waters become blood, (2) frogs, (3) lice, (4) flies, (5) murrain, (6) boils, (7) thunder and hail, (8) locusts, (9) darkness, (10) death of the firstborn 7:20-12:30
8. The Red Sea divided; Israel passes through 14:21-31
9. The waters of Marah sweetened .... Ex. 15:23-25
10. Manna sent daily, except on Sabbath 16:14-35
11. Water from the rock at Rephidim 17:5-7
12. Nadab and Abihu consumed for offering "strange fire" .. Lev. 10:1, 2
13. Some of the people consumed by fire at Taberah .... Num. 11:1-3
14. The earth opens and swallows up Korah and his company; fire and plague follow at Kadesh 16:32
15. Aaron's rod budding at Kadesh 17:8

16. Water from the rock, smitten twice by Moses, Desert of Zin .. 20:7-11
17. The brazen serpent in the Desert of Zin .. Num. 21:8, 9
18. Balaam's ass speaks 22:21-35
19. The Jordan divided, so that Israel passed over dryshod .... Josh. 3:14-17
20. The walls of Jericho fall down .. 6:6-20
21. The sun and moon stayed. Hailstorm 10:12-14
22. The strength of Samson .... Judg 14-16
23. Water from a hollow place "that is in Lehi" 15:19
24. Dagon falls twice before the ark. Emerods on the Philistines ..... 1 Sam. 5:1-12
25. Men of Bethshemesh smitten for looking into the ark 6:19
26. Thunderstorm causes a panic among the Philistines at Ebenezer 7:10-12
27. Thunder and rain in harvest at Gilgal 12:18
28. Sound in the mulberry trees at Rephaim .... 2 Sam. 5:23-25
29. Uzzah smitten for touching the ark at Perezuzzah 6:6, 7
30. Jeroboam's hand withered. His new altar destroyed at Bethel .... 1 Kings 13:4-6
31. Widow of Zarephath's meal and oil increased ... 17:14-16

32. Widow's son raised from the dead 17:17–24

33. Drought, fire, and rain at Elijah's prayer, and Elijah fed by ravens 17, 18

34. Ahaziah's captains consumed by fire near Samaria .... 2 Kings 1:10–12

35. Jordan divided by Elijah and Elisha near Jericho 2:7,8,14

36. Elijah carried up into heaven 2:11

37. Waters of Jericho healed by Elisha's casting salt into them .. 2 Kings 2:21, 22

38. Bears out of the wood destroy forty-two "young men" 2:24

39. Water provided for Jehoshaphat and the allied army 3:16–20

40. The widow's oil multiplied 4:2–7

41. The Shunammite's son given, and raised from the dead at Shunum 4:32–37

42. The deadly pottage cured with meal at Gilgal .. 4:38–41

43. An hundred men fed with twenty loaves at Gilgal 4:42–44

44. Naaman cured of leprosy. Gehazi afflicted with it 5:10–27

45. The iron axehead made to swim, river Jordan 6:5–7

46. Ben-hadad's plans discovered. Hazael's thoughts, etc ... 6:12

47. The Syrian army smitten with blindness at Dothan. 6:18

48. The Syrian army cured of blindness at Samaria 6:20

49. Elisha's bones revive the dead .. 13:21

50. Sennacherib's army destroyed, Jerusalem 19:35

51. Shadow of sun goes back ten degrees on the sundial of Ahaz, Jerusalem 20:9–11

52. Uzziah struck with leprosy, Jerusalem .... 2 Chr. 25:16–21

53. Shadrach, Meshach, and Abednego delivered from the fiery furnace, Babylon .. Dan. 3:10–27

54. Daniel saved in the lions' den .. 6:16–23

55. Jonah in the whale's belly. Safely landed .. Jonah 2:1–10

Parables Recorded in the Old Testament

Spoken By	Concerning	Spoken At	Recorded
Balaam	The Moabites and Israelites	Mount Pisgah	Num. 23:24
Jotham	Trees making a king	Mount Gerizim	Judg 9:7–15
Samson	Sweetness coming forth from the strong	Timnath	Judg. 14:14
Nathan	The poor man's ewe lamb	Jerusalem	2 Sam. 12:1–4
Woman of Tekoah	Two brothers striving	Jerusalem	14:1
One of the sons of the prophets	The escaped prisoner	Near Samaria	1 Kings 20:35–49
Jehoash, king of Israel	The thistle and the cedar	Jerusalem	2 Kings 14:9
Isaiah	The vineyard yielding wild grapes	Jerusalem	Isa. 5:1–6
Ezekiel	Lion's whelps	Babylon	Ezek. 19:2–9
	The great eagles and the vine	Babylon	17:3–10
	The boiling pot	Babylon	24:3–5

Trees and Flowers of the Bible

Almond is the name of two trees mentioned in the Scripture; the one, *Lúz,* translated 'hazel' (A. V.) Gen 30:37, is the wild almond, and the other, *Shaqed,* the cultivated almond, Num 17:8, Gen 43:11, from its early blossoms, a symbol of any sudden interposition, Jer 1:11, and, from their whiteness, of old age, Eccl 12:5.

Almug, or *Algum* (Heb.). Sandal-wood best answers the description in I Ki 10:11,12. The latter name, 2 Ch 2:8 and 9:10,11, is probably an error of transcribers.

Aloes, properly *lign-aloes,* Num 24:6; to be distinguished from the common flowering aloe. The wood is highly odoriferous: see Ps 45:8 Pr 7:17 Ct 4:14 Jn 19:40. Heb. *'Ahalim;* Gr. ἀλόη.

Anise, or dill, occurs only in Mt 23:23 (ἄνηθον). It is an herb of small value. Its seeds are aromatic and carminative, yielding a volatile oil.

Apple. Often thought to be the quince, which is in the East more highly scented, and much sweeter than in Europe; or it may be the apricot, as Dr. Tristram thinks: Pr 25:11 Joel 1:12 Ct 2:3,5 7:8. Heb. *Tappúach.*

Ash, Is 44:14 (A. V.), should properly be fir-tree, as R. V. Heb. *'Oren.*

WORD BIBLE HANDBOOK

Balm. Gen 37:25 Jer 8:22, etc., a medicinal gum, a production of Gilead, probably the *opobalsamum.* Heb. *Tsŏrí.*

Barley. Ex 9:31, etc., the well-known grain. Heb. *Sĕ'orah* (the hairy plant).

Bay-tree only in Ps 37:35; the *Laurus nobilis,* an evergreen with an agreeable spicy odor. But R. V. has 'a tree in its native soil.' Heb. *Ezrach.*

Bean. 2 Sa 17:28 Eze 4:9. Heb. *Bôl.*

Box-tree, the same as that of Europe, though in the East it grows wild and large, Is 41:19 60:13. Specially adapted to mountainous districts, and a calcareous limestone soil, like Lebanon. Heb. *Tĕashshûr.*

Briers. The thorny plants of Palestine are very numerous, and Rabbinical writers say that as many as twenty-two words are used in Scripture to express this species. The particular plants indicated by these words are generally not known, but they are nearly all thorny and useless.

> *Brier, Barqanim,* Judg 8:7,16, some thorny, prickly plant, but sometimes rendered 'threshing instrument,' as Rosenm. *Chedēq,* Pr 15:19 Mic 7:4, 'a brier,' a species of nightshade, *Solanum spinosum* (Royle, Tristram). *Sirpad,* Is 55:13. *Sillon,* Ez 28:24. *Shamîr* (often). *Sarabhim,* Ez 2:6 (the last form not identified).
>
> *Bramble,* Judg 9:14,15, etc. Heb. *'Atād,* by some supposed to be the 'thorn' with which Christ was crowned *(Spina Christi),* properly *thorn,* which see. Also *Choach,* thorn or thistle, which see.
>
> *Bush* (Heb. *Sĕneh*), Ex 3:2 Dt 33:16. The Greek word βάτος means bramble: and the *Rubus sanctus* is common in Palestine.
>
> *Nettle,* Pr 24:31 Job 30:7 Zep 2:9. *Charûl* Royle thinks wild mustard. It is destructive to other vegetation; common to the East; in English, charlock. The nettle is probably the plant mentioned in Is 34:13 Ho 9:6 Pr 24:31 *(Qimmosh),* where it is so translated.
>
> *Thistles,* Gen 3:13, τρίβολος in LXX and New Testament, Mt 7:16 Heb 6:8; a common prickly plant, spreading over the ground. Heb. *Dardar.*
>
> *Thorns,* a general name. Heb. *'Atad,* Ps 58:9, also *bramble;* see above *Choach,* also *thistle,* Job 41:2 Pr 26:9 Is 34:13, and once in pl. *hooks* or *chains,* 2 Ch 33:11 (R. V.). *Chédeq,* also *brier; na'atzútz,* a thorn hedge, Is 55:13. *Mesûbhah,* Mic 7:4. *Sîr,* Eccl 7:6. *Tsēn,* Job 5:5. *Qôts* (collective, often). *Qimmashōn,* Pr 24:31. *Shayith,* Is 5:6, etc. ἄκανθα generally in the LXX; also in Mt 7:16 13:7,22 27:29 Jn 19:2,5.

The number and variety of these words illustrate the abundance of plants of this class in Palestine. The common bramble and the holy bramble *(Rubus sanctus)* abound: and thistles cover large tracts of ground, and grow to a prodigious size; among others, travellers mention the white Syrian thistle, with the Egyptian or purple variety, and the musk-scented thistle *(Carduus mollis).*

Calamus or sweet cane, Ex 30:23 Ct 4:14 Eze 27:19 Is 43:24 Jer 6:20. This plant is found in Asia and Egypt, though the most fragrant are said in Jer to come from a far country. It was one of the ingredients of the anointing oil of the Sanctuary. Heb. *Qaneh.*

Camphire (different from camphor), probably the henna (Gr. κύπρος) of the East: a fragrant shrub, with flowers like those of the lilac. The leaves form a powder used for dyeing the nails and eyebrows, Ct 1;14 4:13. Heb. *Kopher.*

Caper-berry (Eccl 12:5 R. V.), a shrub growing on walls and rocks. The flower-buds, preserved in vinegar, are a stimulating condiment. Heb. *'Abhíyonah.*

Carob-tree, a leguminous shrub found in the countries bordering the Mediterranean, yielding large pods with sweetish seeds, palatable and useful as food for cattle and swine: the 'husks' of Lu 15:16 (Gr. κεράτια).

Cassia, Ex 30:24 Eze 27:19; an inferior kind of cinnamon. The bark yields an essential oil, less aromatic than cinnamon, but in larger quantities, and of a more pungent taste. Heb. *Qiddah, Qĕtsî'oth.*

Cedar, the name generally of coniferous trees, especially of the noblest of the tribe, the cedar of Lebanon. The cedar of the Pentateuch (Lev 14:4,6) was probably a juniper, which tree is common in the desert of Sinai. Heb. *'Erez.*

Chestnut-tree, Gen 30:37 Eze 31:8, probably the plane, *Platanus orientalis,* one of the most magnificent of trees. Those of Assyria were especially fine, see Eze 31. Heb. *'Armôn.*

Cinnamon, Ex 30:23 Pr 7:17 Ct 4:14 Rev 18:13, the bark of the *Laurus kinnamomum.* The plant is found in India and China; but the best kind is from Malabar and Ceylon. Heb. *Qinnamôn.*

Cockle, Job 31:40 (R. V. 'noisome weeds'), perhaps the darnel or 'tares' of the parable, Mt 13:30. The plural is translated 'wild grapes,' Is 5:2. The fruit is narcotic and poisonous. Heb. *Ba'shah.*

Coriander, an umbelliferous plant, yielding a fruit (called seed), the size of a pepper-corn, globular, greyish, and aromatic. It is common in the south of Europe, and is cultivated in Essex, Ex 16:31 Num 11:7. Heb. *Gad.*

Cucumber, Num 11:5 Is 1:8; rightly translated. Extensively cultivated in the East. Heb. *Qishshuim.*

Dove's-dung, 2 Ki 6:25, perhaps the chick-pea, a vetch common in the East. The same name is still applied in Arabic to the dung of pigeons, and to these peas (Bochart, Taylor). Some suppose that the root of a wild-flower, the star of Bethlehem, is the article here mentioned. Heb. *Dibhyonim* (Qĕrî).

Ebony, Eze 27:15, wood greatly prized for its colour and hardness. It is the heart-wood of a date-tree, which grows in great abundance in the East, and especially in Ceylon. Heb. *Hobhnim.*

Fig-tree, properly translated: a native of the East; with broad shady leaves (I Ki 4:25). The fig sprouts at the vernal equinox, and yields three crops of fruit, the first ripening about the end of June, having a fine flavour, and generally eaten green (Jer 24:2). The others are often preserved in masses or cakes, I Sa 25:18, etc. Heb. *Tĕ'ēnah. Pag,* green-fig, cf. 2:13; Gr. σῦκον, συκῆ, freq. in N. T.

Fir-tree is frequently mentioned in Scripture, 2 Sa 6:5 Ct 1:17, etc., and probably includes various coniferous trees. Some regard the cypress and juniper as the true representatives of *berosh;* others the cedar, and others the common pine. All are found in Palestine; and as cedar and fir constantly occur together in Scripture, they probably include the whole genus. Heb. *Bĕrosh.*

Fitches, i.e. vetches, occurs only in Is 28:25,27, and is probably a species of *Nigella* (black cummin, R. V. *marg.*). The seeds are black, and are used in the East, like carraway seeds, for the purpose of imparting to food an aromatic, acrid taste. Heb. *Qetzach.*

Flag (translated meadow, in Gen 41:2,18) Job 8:11, probably any green herbaceous plants of luxuriant growth. Heb. *'Achu.*

Flax (*Pishtah,* once translated 'tow,' Is 43:17, more properly 'a wick'): the common plant so called, used to make linen, cord, and torches; extensively cultivated in Egypt and Syria. Gr. λίνον, Mt 12:20.

Shēsh, translated fine linen and silk, was probably the *hemp* plant, in Arabic *hasheesh,* yielding an intoxicating drink (whence assassin), now known as the *bang* of the East. The plant is cultivated in Persia, Europe, and India.

Three other words are translated linen in the English version, *Badh, Bûts,* and *Sadîn,* the first in the Pentateuch, etc., and is probably the *linen* made from flax; the second only in Chronicles and the Prophets, and is probably *cotton* cloth, a product not mentioned till after the Captivity: it is generally translated 'fine linen'; the third only in Pr 31:24 Is 3:23 'linen raiment.' The βύσσος of the New Testament was probably linen. In the LXX, βύσσος represents both words, *Badh* and *Bûts;* for*Sadin,* σινδών is used (see Mt 27:50 and parallels). The word *cotton* does not occur in Scripture, but the Hebrew *Karpas,* in Est 1:6, is translated *green* (A. V.) and *cotton* (R. V.). The cotton plant seems not to have been known in Palestine before the Captivity.

Galbanum, Ex 30:34 only, a very powerful and not very fragrant gum, exuded by a shrub belonging to the family of Umbelliferæ. It was used in preparing incense. Heb. *Chelbĕnah.*

Garlick, Num 11:5 only. This plant is now known by the name of eschalot, or shalot, and is common in Europe (*Allium Escalonium,* i. e. of Ascalon). Herodotus states that it was supplied in large quantities to the labourers engaged in the erection of the Pyramids. Heb. *Shûm.*

Gopher is mentioned only in Gen 6:14. Probably a tree of the pine tribe, perhaps cypress, which is very abundant in Assyria. Heb. *Gopher.*

Gourd, Jon 4:6–10, Heb., *Qiqayôn,* is now generally admitted to be the *Palma Christi,* or castor-oil plant. It is of very rapid growth, with broad palmate leaves, and giving, especially when young, an ample shade. The oil is obtained from the seeds of the tree.

Gourd, wild, 2 Ki 4:39. Heb. pl. *Paqqu'oth.* The wild cucumber, whose leaves are like those of the vine, but of a poisonous quality and bitter taste.

Hemlock, Ho 10:4. Heb. *Rōsh.* Translated 'gall' in Dt 29:18 Ps 69:21 Lam 3:19, etc. Probably a general name for any bitter herb (Heb. *La'anah* 'wormwood').

Hyssop, Ex 12:22 Jn 19:29, etc., either marjoram, a small shrub, its leaves covered with soft woolly down, adapted to retain fluid; or the thorny caper, which grows wild in Syria, and is possessed of detergent properties. Heb. '*Ezôbh,* Gr. ὕσσωπος.

Juniper, I Ki 19:4,5 Ps 120:4; probably the Spanish broom. The wood of this tree burns with a remarkably light flame, giving out great heat: hence 'coals of juniper' in Ps 120 (and R. V. marg. Job 30:4, 'to warm them'). Heb. *Rothem.*

Leeks, Num 11:5. The word so translated is rendered 'grass,' I Ki 18:5; 'herb,' Job 8:12; and 'hay,' Pr 27:25. It properly means anything green. But it is translated 'leeks' in these passages by most of the versions; and the plant has been known (and indeed worshipped) in Egypt from very early times. Heb. *Chatsîr.*

Lentiles, a kind of pulse, from a small annual, and used for making soups and pottage. It is of the colour of chocolate (reddish-brown), and is compared by Pliny to the colour of the reddish sand around the pyramids. Wilkinson *(Ancient Egypt)* has given a picture of lentile-pottage making, taken from an ancient slab. Gen 25:34 2 Sa 17:28. Heb. '*Adashim.*

Lily. This word is probably applicable to several plants common in Palestine. In most passages of Scripture where the word is used, there is reference to the lotus, or water-lily of the Nile. This species was eaten as food: the roots, stalks, and seeds are all very grateful, both fresh and dried. Hence the allusion to feeding among lilies. The 'lily of the valley,' i. e. of the water-courses, belongs also to this species, Ct 2:2,16 4:5, etc. The flower was worn on festive occasions, and formed one of the ornaments of the Temple, I Ki 7:19. Heb. *Shûshân.*

The lily of the New Testament (κρίνον) is the scarlet martagon lily *(Lil. chalcedonicum),* a stately turban-like flower. It flowers in April and May, when the Sermon on the Mount was probably delivered, and is indigenous throughout Galilee. It is called in the New Testament the 'lily of the field,' Mt 6:28.

Mallows, only in Job 30:4, R. V. 'salt-wort,' *Atriplex halimus;* is still used by the poor as a common dish. Heb. *Mallûach.*

Mandrakes, Gen 30:14,16 Ct 7:13, *Atropa mandragora,* a plant like lettuce in size and shape, but of dark green leaves. The fruit is of the size of a small apple, and ripens in wheat-harvest (May). It is noted for its exhilarating and genial virtues. Heb. *Dudaim.*

Melon, Num 11:5. The gourd tribe, to which cucumbers and melons belong, are great favourites in the East, and abound in Egypt and India. There are different kinds—the Egyptian *(Cucumis chate),* the common watermelon, etc., all of which are probably included in the Scripture name. Heb. '*Abhattichim.*

Millet, Eze 4:9, the *Panicum miliaceum* of botanists, a small grain sometimes cultivated in England for feeding poultry, and grown throughout the East. It is used for food in Persia and in India. Heb. *Dochan.*

Mulberry, in the New Testament, *sycamine*-tree, Lu 17:6 (very different from the *sycomore,* which is a kind of fig), is the mulberry of Europe, very common in Palestine. The word translated 'mulberry' in 2 Sa 5:23,24 I Ch 14:14,15 probably means *balsam-tree.* The rustling of its leaves answers the description given in these passages. The same word occurs in Ps 84:6, and is there regarded (A. V.) as a proper name *(Baca)*, but most of the versions (as R. V.) translate it 'weeping.' Valley of Baca = 'vale of tears.'

Mustard is either a species of the plant known in England under this name, which has one of the smallest seeds, and is itself among the tallest of herbaceous plants, or the *Salvadora Persica*, a shrub or tree, whose seeds are used for the same purpose as mustard (Royle, Irby).

Myrrh is the representative of two words in Hebrew, of which the first *(Môr, σμύρνα)* is properly translated, Ex 30:23 Ps 45:8, etc. Jn 19:39. It is a gum exuded by the *Balsamodendron myrrha*, and other plants. It is highly aromatic and medicinal, and moderately stimulating. The Greeks used it to drug their wine. The shrub is found in Arabia and Africa.

> *Bĕdolach*, Gen 2:12 Num 11:7, is probably a gum, still known as *bdellium*. The gum exudes from more than one tree, and is found in both India and Africa.

> *Lôt* is properly labdanum. It is a gum exuded by the cistus, and is now used chiefly in fumigation, Gen 37:25 43:11. Other similar gums mentioned in Scripture are—

> *Balm (Tsŏrí)*, Gen 37:25 Jer 8:22. It is probably the balm or balsam of Gilead (the Hebrew of which word, however, *Bésem*, is generally translated *spice*, or *sweet odors*). This tree is common in Arabia and Africa. The gum is obtained in small quantities, and is highly aromatic and medicinal.

> *Frankincense (Lèbhonah)*, is a gum taken from a species of storax, and is highly fragrant. It was employed chiefly for fumigation, and was largely used in the service of the Temple. It was regarded as an emblem of prayer, Lev 2:1 Ps 145:1,2 Rev 8:3,4.

> *Spicery (Nĕkh'oth)*, Gen 37:25 43:11, is a kind of gum, perhaps taken from the tragacanth tree.

> *Stacte (Nātāph)*, occurs only in Ex 30:34, and is another gum, not now certainly known. Celsius thinks in an inferior kind of myrrh.

Myrtle grows wild in Palestine, and reaches the height of twenty feet. Its leaves are dark and glossy, and its white flowers highly aromatic. Its branches were used at the Feast of Tabernacles, Ne 8:18 Is 41:17–19. Heb. *Hădhas.*

Nard, Mk 14:3. Heb. *Nērd*, Gr. νάρδος, translated *spikenard*, the Indian plant *Nardostachys jatamansi*, yielding a delicious and costly perfume. The root and the leaves that grow out of it have the appearance of spikes, hence the name *(stachys = spike)*. Mk 14:3; Jan 12:3.

Nut is the translation of two Hebrew words: *Botnim*, Gen 43:11, pistachio-nuts, well known in Syria and India, but not in Egypt, and *'Eghoz*, the walnut-tree, Ct 6:11, which is called in Pers. and Arab. 'gouz.'

Oak, Gen 35:8 Is 2:13 6:13 44:14 Eze 27:6 Ho 4:13 Amos 2:9 Zec 11:2. In other passages where the word 'oak' is found, the word ought to be *terebinth*, or turpentine-tree (see *teil*). The oak is not common in Palestine, nor is the English oak *(Quercus robur)* found there. Oaks of Bashan are still of large size; but they are chiefly either the evergreen oak *(Q. ilex)*, the prickly-cupped oak *(Q. valonia)*, or the Kermes oak. Heb *'Allon.*

Olive, an evergreen, common from Italy to Cabul. The unripe fruit is preserved in a solution of salt, and is used for dessert; when ripe, it is bruised in mills, and yields an oil of peculiar purity and value. Both the oil and the tree were used in the Feast of Tabernacles. In Judæa it was a symbol of prosperity, Ps 52:8, and in all ages it has been an emblem of peace.

The wild olive (Ro 11:17,24) was probably a wild species of the *Olea Europœa.* It was a common mode of grafting in Italy, to insert a branch of the wild olive in the stock of the cultivated plant *(Columella).* Heb. *Zayith,* Gr. ἐλαία.

Onion, a plant well known in this country and in the East. In hot climates it loses its acrid taste, and is highly agreeable and nutritious, Num 11:5. Heb. *Bétzel.*

Palm, or date-tree, is one of the most valuable eastern trees, Ex 15:27. It flourished especially in the valley of Jordan (hence Jericho, the City of Palm-trees) and in the deserts of Syria (*Tamar* = Palmyra). It was considered characteristic of Judæa, being first met with there by nations traveling southward from Europe. Heb. *Tāmār,* Gr. φοίνιξ, whence Phœnicia.

Pomegranate ('grained-apple'), a tree of great value in hot climates. Its fruit is globular, and as large as a good-sized apple. The interior contains a quantity of purple or rosy seeds, with a sweet juice, of a slightly acid taste, I Sa 14:2. The tree is not unlike the common hawthorn, but larger. It is cultivated in North Africa and throughout Asia. Hag 2:19 Dt 8:8 Ct 8:2 Joel 1:12. Heb. *Rimmon.*

Carved pomegrantes were placed on the capitals of the columns of the Temple, Ex 28:33,34.

Poplar, Ho 4:13, is either the white poplar or the storax-tree, Gen 30:37, LXX, and R. V. marg. The latter yields the fragrant resin of frankincense. Either tree answers the description given in Genesis and Hosea. Heb. *Libhneh.*

Reed, a tall, grassy plant, consisting of a long, hollow-jointed stem, with sharp-cutting leaves. The plant grows on the banks of rivers and in moist places, I Ki 14:15 Job 40:21 Is 19:6,7 36:6 Ex 40:5 Mt 11:7, and was used for measuring, fishing, walking, etc.

A small kind was used for writing, 3 Jn 13. This reed is very abundant in the marshes between the Tigris and the Euphrates. Heb. *Qaneh,* Gr. κάλαμος.

Rose, Ct 2:1 Is 35:1. Though the rose was known in Syria, the dogrose being common on the mountains, and the damask rose taking its name from Damascus, it is not mentioned in Scripture; the word so translated being (as its name imples) a bulbous-rooted plant. It is probably the sweet narcissus, abundant in the plain of Sharon, in fact the characteristic wild flower of the district. Heb. *Chăvatzéleth.*

Rue, only in Lu 11:42, is the common garden-plant so called. Its leaves emit a strong and bitter odor, and were formerly used medicinally. Gr. πήγανον.

Rush, Ex 2:3 Is 9:14 19:15, translated also 'hook,' Job 41:2 ('rope of rushes,'

R. V. marg.) and 'bulrush,' Is 58:5 (A. V.), the Egyptian *papyrus,* Is 18:2 (R. V.), which belongs to the tribe, not of rushes, but of sedges. It grows eight or ten feet high. The stem is triangular, and without leaves, but is adorned with a large, flocculent, bushy top. The plant was used for making boats, sails, mats, and ropes; the stem itself yielding the celebrated paper of Egypt. The plant is found in all parts of the Nile, near Babylon, and in India. Heb. *Gomē, Agmôn.*

Saffron, Ct 4:14. The stigmas and style of the yellow crocus formed this fragrant perfume, which was used to flavour both meat and wine, and as a powerful stimulative medicine. It is very common throughout Asia, and derives its English name from the Arabic *'zafran.'* Heb. *Karkōm.*

Shittah-tree, the acacia, or Egyptian thorn, Ex 25:5, etc. The stem is straight and thorny, the bark is a grayish-black, the wood very light and durable, and therefore well adapted for a movable structure like the Tabernacle. All this species bear flowers, and are remarkable for their fragrance and beauty. Heb. plur. *Shittîm.*

Sycomore, I Ki 10:27 Ps 78:47, etc., erroneously translated by the LXX συκάμινος (see Mulberry). In its leaves it resembles the mulberry, but is really a fig-tree, bearing a coarse, inferior fruit *(Ficus sycomorus).* It is lofty and shady (Lu 19:4), with wood of no great value (I Ki 10:27 2 Ch 1:15). The mummy-cases of Egypt were generally made of it. Heb. *Shiqmah.* This tree must be distinguished from the English sycamore, which is a kind of maple.

Tares (ζιζάνια), Mt 13:25, the *Lolium temulentum,* a kind of darnel, or grass, resembling wheat until the seeds appear. It impoverishes the soil, and bears a seed of deleterious properties.

Teil-tree, Is 6:13, an old English name for the 'lime-tree,' which is not found in Palestine. The R. V. rightly has 'terebinth' in the above passage. So has R. V. for A. V. 'elm' in Ho 4:13, and for 'oak' in Gen 35:4 marg. and in other passages. See Oak. It is also known as the turpentine-tree, from the fragrant substance exuding from its bark. Heb. *Elah.*

Thyine-wood, Rev 18:12, was in great demand among the Romans, who called it thya, or citron-wood. It grows only in the neighborhood of Mount Atlas, in Africa, and yields the 'sandarach' rosin of commerce. It is highly balsamic and odoriferous.

Vine, Gen 9:20, etc., a well-known tree, and highly esteemed throughout the East. The vine of Eshcol was especially celebrated, Num 13:23,24. The vine was grown on terraces on the hills of Palestine, Is 5:1 Mic 1:6, or elsewhere on the ground, Eze 17:6,7. Sometimes it formed an arbor, I Ki 4:25 Ho 2:12, propped up and trained. Often metaphorically used, as in Jn 15. A noble vine = men of generous disposition, Jer 2:21. A strange, or wild vine = men ignoble and degenerate, Dt 32:32, etc. Heb. *Géphen* (also *Sorēq,* yielding rich red or purple grapes, Is 5:2 Jer 2:4 Gen 49:11, also denoting the valley that produced them, Judg 16:4), Gr. ἄμπελος.

Willow, Ps 137:2 Is 44:4, was well known in Judæa, and one species, the weeping willow, is the *Salix Babylonica.* Heb. *'Erebh. Tsaphtsāphah,* Ez 17:5, is probably the Egyptian willow *(Salix Ægyptiaca).*

Wormwood, 'root of bitterness,' Dt 29:17 Rev 8:10,11, an emblem of trouble.

There are various species of this tribe *(Artemisia)*, of which the English plant *(A. absinthium)* is a specimen. Several kinds are found in Judæa, all exceedingly bitter. The wormwood of commerce consists of the tops of the plants, flowers, and young seeds intermixed. Heb. *La'ănah*, Gr. ἀψίνθιον.

SUBJECT INDEX

We use a concordance as a tool to find every occurrence of words used in the Bible; this index is not a concordance. Instead the index is designed to help you locate Handbook discussions of the significant topics listed. The most significant discussions are indicated by page numbers in parentheses ( ).